The
Beautiful Lady

Booth Tarkington

1st WORLD
LIBRARY
Literary Society

The Beautiful Lady

Booth Tarkington

© 1st World Library – Literary Society, 2005
PO Box 2211
Fairfield, IA 52556
www.1stworldlibrary.org
First Edition

LCCN: 2004195585

Softcover ISBN: 1-4218-0406-9
Hardcover ISBN: 1-4218-0306-2
eBook ISBN: 1-4218-0506-5

Purchase *"The Beautiful Lady"*
as a traditional bound book at:
www.1stWorldLibrary.org/purchase.asp?ISBN=1-4218-0406-9

1st World Library Literary Society is a nonprofit
organization dedicated to promoting literacy by:

- Creating a free internet library accessible from any computer worldwide.
- Hosting writing competitions and offering book publishing scholarships.

Readers interested in supporting literacy
through sponsorship, donations or
membership please contact:
literacy@1stworldlibrary.org
Check us out at: www.1stworldlibrary.ORG
and start downloading free ebooks today.

The Beautiful Lady
contributed by Tim, Ed & Rodney
in support of
1st World Library Literary Society

CHAPTER ONE

Nothing could have been more painful to my sensitiveness than to occupy myself, confused with blushes, at the center of the whole world as a living advertisement of the least amusing ballet in Paris.

To be the day's sensation of the boulevards one must possess an eccentricity of appearance conceived by nothing short of genius; and my misfortunes had reduced me to present such to all eyes seeking mirth. It was not that I was one of those people in uniform who carry placards and strange figures upon their backs, nor that my coat was of rags; on the contrary, my whole costume was delicately rich and well chosen, of soft grey and fine linen (such as you see worn by a marquis in the pe'sage at Auteuil) according well with my usual air and countenance, sometimes esteemed to resemble my father's, which were not wanting in distinction.

To add to this my duties were not exhausting to the body. I was required only to sit without a hat from ten of the morning to midday, and from four until seven in the afternoon, at one of the small tables under the awning of the Cafe' de la Paix at the corner of the Place de l'Opera - that is to say, the centre of the inhabited world. In the morning I drank my coffee, hot in the cup; in the afternoon I sipped it cold in the glass. I spoke to no one; not a glance or a gesture of mine passed to attract notice.

Yet I was the centre of that centre of the world. All day the crowds surrounded me, laughing loudly; all the voyous making those jokes for which I found no repartee. The pavement was sometimes blocked; the passing coachmen stood up in their boxes to look over at me, small infants were elevated on shoulders to behold me; not the gravest or most sorrowful came by without stopping to gaze at me and go away with rejoicing faces. The boulevards rang to their laughter - all Paris laughed!

For seven days I sat there at the appointed times, meeting the eye of nobody, and lifting my coffee with fingers which trembled with embarrassment at this too great conspicuosity! Those mournful hours passed, one by the year, while the idling bourgeois and the travellers made ridicule; and the rabble exhausted all effort to draw plays of wit from me.

I have told you that I carried no placard, that my costume was elegant, my demeanour modest in all degree.

"How, then, this excitement?" would be your disposition to inquire. "Why this sensation?"

It is very simple. My hair had been shaved off, all over my ears, leaving only a little above the back of the neck, to give an appearance of far-reaching baldness, and on my head was painted, in ah! so brilliant letters of distinctness:

Theatre
Folie-Rouge

Booth Tarkington

Revue
de
Printemps
Tous les Soirs

Such was the necessity to which I was at that time reduced! One has heard that the North Americans invent the most singular advertising, but I will not believe they surpass the Parisian. Myself, I say I cannot express my sufferings under the notation of the crowds that moved about the Cafe' de la Paix! The French are a terrible people when they laugh sincerely. It is not so much the amusing things which cause them amusement; it is often the strange, those contrasts which contain something horrible, and when they laugh there is too frequently some person who is uncomfortable or wicked. I am glad that I was born not a Frenchman; I should regret to be native to a country where they invent such things as I was doing in the Place de l'Opera; for, as I tell you, the idea was not mine.

As I sat with my eyes drooping before the gaze of my terrible and applauding audiences, how I mentally formed cursing words against the day when my misfortunes led me to apply at the Theatre Folie-Rouge for work! I had expected an audition and a role of comedy in the Revue; for, perhaps lacking any experience of the stage, I am a Neapolitan by birth, though a resident of the Continent at large since the age of fifteen. All Neapolitans can act; all are actors; comedians of the greatest, as every traveller is cognizant. There is a thing in the air of our beautiful slopes which makes the people of a great instinctive musicalness and deceptiveness, with passions like those burning in the old mountain we have there. They are ready to play, to sing - or to explode, yet, imitating that amusing Vesuvio, they never do this last when you are in expectancy, or, as a spectator, hopeful of it.

How could any person wonder, then, that I, finding myself suddenly destitute in Paris, should apply at the theatres? One after another, I saw myself no farther than the director's door, until (having had no more to eat the day preceding than three green almonds, which I took from a cart while the good female was not looking) I reached the Folie-Rouge. Here I was astonished to find a polite reception from the director. It eventuated that they wished for a person appearing like myself a person whom they would outfit with clothes of quality in all parts, whose external presented a gentleman of the great world, not merely of one the galant-uomini, but who would impart an air to a table at a cafe' where he might sit and partake. The contrast of this with the emplacement of the establishment on his bald head-top was to be the success of the idea. It was plain that I had no baldness, my hair being very thick and I but twenty-four years of age, when it was explained that my hair could be shaved. They asked me to accept, alas! not a part in the Revue, but a specialty as a sandwich-man. Knowing the English tongue as I do, I may afford the venturesomeness to play upon it a little: I asked for bread, and they offered me not a role, but a sandwich!

It must be undoubted that I possessed not the disposition to make any fun with my accomplishments during those days that I spent under the awning of the Cafe' de la Paix. I had consented to be the advertise-ment in greatest desperation, and not considering what the reality would be. Having consented, honour compelled that I fulfil to the ending. Also, the costume and outfittings I wore were part of my emolument. They had been constructed for me by the finest tailor; and though I had impulses, often, to leap up and fight through the noisy ones about me and run far to the open country, the very garments I wore were fetters binding me to remain and suffer. It seemed to me that the hours were spent not in the centre of a ring of human persons, but of un-well-made pantaloons and ugly skirts. Yet all of these pantaloons and skirts had such scrutinous eyes and expressions of mirth to laugh like demons at my conscious, burning, painted head; eyes which spread out, astonished at the sight of me, and peered and winked and grinned from the big wrinkles above the gaiters of Zouaves, from the red breeches of the gendarmes, the knickerbockers of the cyclists, the white ducks of sergents de ville, and the knees of the boulevardiers, bagged with sitting cross-legged at the little tables. I could not escape these eyes; - how scornfully they twinkled at me from the spurred and glittering officers' boots! How with amaze from the American and English trousers, both turned up and creased like folded paper, both with some dislike for each other but for all other trousers more.

It was only at such times when the mortifications to appear so greatly embarrassed became stronger than the embarrassment itself that I could by will power force my head to a straight construction and look out upon my spectators firmly. On the second day of my ordeal, so facing the laughers, I found myself facing straight into the monocle of my half-brother and ill-wisher, Prince Caravacioli.

At this, my agitation was sudden and very great, for there was no one I wished to prevent perceiving my condition more than that old Antonio Caravacioli! I had not known that he was in Paris, but I could have no doubt it was himself: the monocle, the handsome nose, the toupee', the yellow skin, the dyed-black moustache, the splendid height - it was indeed Caravacioli! He was costumed for the automobile, and threw but one glance at me as he crossed the pavement to his car, which was in waiting. There was no change, not of the faintest, in that frosted tragic mask of a countenance, and I was glad to think that he had not recognized me.

And yet, how strange that I should care, since all his life he had declined to recognize me as what I was! Ah, I should have been glad to shout his age, his dyes, his artificialities, to all the crowd, so to touch him where it would most pain him! For was he not the vainest man in the whole world? How well I knew his vulnerable point: the monstrous depth of his vanity in that pretense of youth which he preserved through superhuman pains and a genius of a valet, most excellently! I had much to pay Antonio for myself, more for my father, most for my mother. This was why that last of all the world I would have wished that old fortune-hunter to know how far I had been reduced!

Then I rejoiced about that change which my unreal baldness produced in me, giving me a look of forty years instead of twenty-four, so that my oldest friend must take at least three stares to know me. Also, my costume would disguise me from the few acquaintances I had in Paris (if they chanced to cross the Seine), as they had only seen me in the shabbiest; while, at my last meeting with Antonio, I had been as fine in the coat as now.

Yet my encouragement was not so joyful that my gaze lifted often. On the very last day, in the afternoon when my observances were most and noisiest, I lifted my eyes but once during the final half-hour - but such a one that was!

The edge of that beautiful grey pongee skirt came upon the lid of my lowered eyelid like a cool shadow over hot sand. A sergent had just made many of the people move away, so there remained only a thin ring of the laughing pantaloons about me, when this divine skirt presented its apparition to me. A pair of North-American trousers accompanied it, turned up to show the ankle-bones of a rich pair of stockings; neat, enthusiastic and humorous, I judged them to be; for, as one may discover, my only amusement during my martyrdom - if this misery can be said to possess such alleviatings - had been the study of feet, pantaloons, and skirts. The trousers in this case detained my observation no time. They were but the darkest corner of the chiaroscuro of a Rembrandt - the mellow glow of gold was all across the grey skirt.

How shall I explain myself, how make myself understood? Shall I be thought sentimentalistic or but mad when I declare that my first sight of the grey pongee skirt caused me a thrill of excitation, of tenderness, and - oh-i-me! - of self-consciousness more acute than all my former mortifications. It was so very different from all other skirts that had shown them-selves to me those sad days, and you may understand that, though the pantaloons far outnumbered the skirts, many hundreds of the latter had also been objects of my gloomy observation.

This skirt, so unlike those which had passed, presented at once the qualifications of its superiority. It had been constructed by an artist, and it was worn by a lady. It did not pine, it did not droop; there was no more an atom of hanging too much than there was a portion inflated by flamboyancy; it did not assert itself; it bore notice without seeking it. Plain but exquisite, it was that great rarity - goodness made charming.

The peregrination of the American trousers suddenly stopped as they caught sight of me, and that precious skirt paused, precisely in opposition to my little table. I heard a voice, that to which the skirt pertained. It spoke the English, but not in the manner of the inhabitants of London, who seem to sing undistin-guishably in their talking, although they are comprehensible to each other. To an Italian it seems that many North-Americans and English seek too often the assistance of the nose in talking, though in different manners, each equally unagreeable to our ears. The intelligent among our lazzaroni of Naples, who beg from tourists, imitate this, with the purpose of reminding the generous traveller of his home, in such a way to soften his heart. But there is some difference: the Italian, the Frenchman, or German who learns English sometimes misunderstands the American: the Englishman he sometimes understands.

This voice that spoke was North-American. Ah, what a voice! Sweet as the mandolins of Sorento! Clear as the bells of Capri! To hear it, was like coming upon sight of the almond-blossoms of Sicily for the first time, or the tulip-fields of Holland. Never before was such a voice!

"Why did you stop, Rufus?" it said.

"Look!" replied the American trousers; so that I knew the pongee lady had not observed me of herself.

Instantaneously there was an exclamation, and a pretty grey parasol, closed, fell at my feet. It is not the pleasantest to be an object which causes people to be startled when they behold you; but I blessed the agitation of this lady, for what caused her parasol to fall from her hand was a start of pity.

"Ah!" she cried. "The poor man!"

She had perceived that I was a gentleman.

I bent myself forward and lifted the parasol, though not my eyes I could not have looked up into the face above me to be Caesar! Two hands came down into the circle of my observation; one of these was that belonging to the trousers, thin, long, and white; the other was the grey-gloved hand of the lady, and never had I seen such a hand - the hand of an angel in a suede glove, as the grey skirt was the mantle of a saint made by Doucet. I speak of saints and angels; and to the large world these may sound like cold words. - It is only in Italy where some people are found to adore them still.

I lifted the parasol toward that glove as I would have moved to set a candle on an altar. Then, at a thought, I placed it not in the glove, but in the thin hand of the gentleman. At the same time the voice of the lady spoke to me - I was to have the joy of remembering that this voice had spoken four words to me.

"Je vous remercie, monsieur," it said.

"Pas de quoi!" I murmured.

The American trousers in a loud tone made reference in the idiom to my miserable head: "Did you ever see anything to beat it?"

The beautiful voice answered, and by the gentleness of her sorrow for me I knew she had no thought that I might understand. "Come away. It is too pitiful!"

Then the grey skirt and the little round-toed shoes beneath it passed from my sight, quickly hidden from me by the increasing crowd; yet I heard the voice a moment more, but fragmentarily: "Don't you see how ashamed he is, how he must have been starving before he did that, or that someone dependent on him needed -"

I caught no more, but the sweetness that this beautiful lady understood and felt for the poor absurd wretch was so great that I could have wept. I had not seen her face; I had not looked up - even when she went.

"Who is she?" cried a scoundrel voyous, just as she turned. "Madame of the parasol? A friend of monsieur of the ornamented head?"

"No. It is the first lady in waiting to his wife, Madame la Duchesse," answered a second. "She has been sent with an equerry to demand of monseigneur if he does not wish a little sculpture upon his dome as well as the colour decorations!"

"'Tis true, my ancient?" another asked of me.

I made no repartee, continuing to sit with my chin dependent upon my cravat, but with things not the same in my heart as formerly to the arrival of that grey pongee, the grey glove, and the beautiful voice.

Since King Charles the Mad, in Paris no one has been completely free from lunacy while the spring-time is happening. There is something in the sun and the banks of the Seine. The Parisians drink sweet and fruity champagne because the good wines are already in their veins. These Parisians are born intoxicated and remain so; it is not fair play to require them to be like other human people. Their deepest feeling is for the arts; and, as everyone had declared, they are farceurs in their tragedies, tragic in their comedies. They prepare the last epigram in the tumbril; they drown themselves with enthusiasm about the alliance with Russia. In death they are witty; in war they have poetic spasms; in love they are mad.

The strangest of all this is that it is not only the Parisians who are the insane ones in Paris; the visitors are none of them in behaviour as elsewhere. You have only to go there to become as lunatic as the rest. Many travellers, when they have departed, remember the events they have caused there as a person remembers in the morning what he has said and thought in the moonlight of the night.

In Paris it is moonlight even in the morning; and in Paris one falls in love even more strangely than by moonlight.

It is a place of glimpses: a veil fluttering from a motor-car, a little lace handkerchief fallen from a victoria, a figure crossing a lighted window, a black hat vanishing in the distance of the avenues of the Tuileries. A young man writes a ballade and dreams over a bit of lace. Was I not, then, one of the least extravagant of this mad people? Men have fallen in love with photographs, those greatest of liars; was I so wild, then, to

adore this grey skirt, this small shoe, this divine glove,
the golden-honey voice - of all in Paris the only one to
pity and to understand? Even to love the mystery of
that lady and to build my dreams upon it? - to love all
the more because of the mystery? Mystery is the last
word and the completing charm to a young man's
passion. Few sonnets have been written to wives
whose matrimony is more than five years of age - is it
not so?

CHAPTER TWO

When my hour was finished and I in liberty to leave that horrible corner, I pushed out of the crowd and walked down the boulevard, my hat covering my sin, and went quickly. To be in love with my mystery, I thought, that was a strange happiness! It was enough. It was romance! To hear a voice which speaks two sentences of pity and silver is to have a chime of bells in the heart. But to have a shaven head is to be a monk! And to have a shaven head with a sign painted upon it is to be a pariah. Alas! I was a person whom the Parisians laughed at, not with!

Now that at last my martyrdom was concluded, I had some shuddering, as when one places in his mouth a morsel of unexpected flavour. I wondered where I had found the courage to bear it, and how I had resisted hurling myself into the river, though, as is known, that is no longer safe, for most of those who attempt it are at once rescued, arrested, fined, and imprisoned for throwing bodies into the Seine, which is forbidden.

At the theatre the frightful badge was removed from my head-top and I was given three hundred francs, the price of my shame, refusing an offer to repeat the performance during the following week. To imagine such a thing made me a choking in my throat, and I left the bureau in some sickness. This increased so much (as I approached the Madeleine, where I wished to mount an omnibus) that I entered a restaurant and drank a small glass of cognac. Then I called for writing-papers and wrote to the good Mother Superior and my dear little nieces at their convent. I enclosed two hundred and fifty francs, which sum I had fallen behind in my payments for their education and sustenance, and I felt a moment's happiness that at least for a while I need not fear that my poor brother's orphans might become objects of charity - a fear which, accompanied by my own hunger, had led me to become the joke of the boulevards.

Feeling rich with my remaining fifty francs, I ordered the waiter to bring me a goulasch and a carafe of blond beer, after the consummation of which I spent an hour in the reading of a newspaper. Can it be credited that the journal of my perusement was the one which may be called the North-American paper of the aristocracies of Europe? Also, it contains some names of the people of the United States at the hotels and elsewhere.

How eagerly I scanned those singular columns! Shall I confess to what purpose? I read the long lists of uncontinental names over and over, but I lingered not at all upon those like "Muriel," "Hermione," "Violet," and "Sibyl," nor over "Balthurst," "Skeffington-Sligo," and "Covering-Legge"; no, my search was for the Sadies and Mamies, the Thompsons, Van Dusens, and Bradys. In that lies my preposterous secret.

You will see to what infatuation those words of pity, that sense of a beautiful presence, had led me. To fall in love must one behold a face? Yes; at thirty. At twenty, when one is something of a poet - No: it is sufficient to see a grey pongee skirt! At fifty, when one is a philosopher - No: it is enough to perceive a soul! I had done both; I had seen the skirt; I had perceived the soul! Therefore, while hungry, I neglected my goulasch to read these lists of names of the United States again and again, only that I might have the thought that one of them - though I knew not which - might be this lady's, and that in so infinitesimal a degree I had been near her again. Will it be estimated extreme imbecility in me when I ventured the additional confession that I felt a great warmth and tenderness toward the possessors of all these names, as being, if not herself, at least her compatriots?

I am now brought to the admission that before to-day I had experienced some prejudices against the inhabitants of the North-American republic, though not on account of great experience of my own. A year previously I had made a disastrous excursion to Monte Carlo in the company of a young gentleman of London who had been for several weeks in New York and Washington and Boston, and appeared to know very much of the country. He was never anything but tired in speaking of it, and told me a great amount. He said many times that in the hotels there was never a concierge or portier to give you information where to discover the best vaudeville; there was no concierge at all! In New York itself, my friend told me, a facchino, or species of porter, or some such good-for-nothing, had said to him, including a slap on the shoulder, "Well, brother, did you receive your delayed luggage correctly?" (In this instance my studies of the North-American idiom lead me to believe that my friend was intentionally truthful in regard to the principalities, but mistaken in his observation of detail.) He declared the recent willingness of the English to take some interest in the United-Statesians to be a mistake; for their were noisy, without real confidence in themselves; they were restless and merely imitative instead of inventive. He told me that he was not exceptional; all Englishmen had thought similarly for fifty or sixty years; therefore, naturally, his opinion carried great weight with me. And myself, to my astonishment, I had often seen parties of these republicans become all ears and whispers when somebody called a prince or a countess passed by. Their reverence for age itself, in anything but a horse, had often surprised me by its artlessness, and of all strange things in the world, I have heard them admire old customs and old families. It was strange to me to listen, when I had believed that their land was the only one where happily no person need worry to remember who had been his great-grand-father.

The greatest of my own had not saved me from the decoration of the past week, yet he was as much mine as he was Antonio Caravacioli's; and Antonio, though impoverished, had his motor-car and dined well, since I happened to see, in my perusal of the journal, that he had been to dinner the evening before at the English Embassy with a great company. "Bravo, Antonio! Find a rich foreign wife if you can, since you cannot do well for yourself at home!" And I could say so honestly, without spite, for all his hatred of me, - because, until I had paid my addition, I was still the possessor of fifty francs!

Fifty francs will continue life in the body of a judicial person a long time in Paris, and combining that knowledge and the good goulasch, I sought diligently for "Mamies" and "Sadies" with a revived spirit. I found neither of those adorable names - in fact, only two such diminutives, which are more charming than our Italian ones: A Miss Jeanie Archibald Zip and a Miss Fannie Sooter. None of the names was harmonious with the grey pongee - in truth, most of them were no prettier (however less processional) than royal names. I could not please myself that I had come closer to the rare lady; I must be contented that the same sky covered us both, that the noise of the same city rang in her ears as mine.

Yet that was a satisfaction, and to know that it was true gave me mysterious breathlessness and made me hear fragments of old songs during my walk that night. I walked very far, under the trees of the Bois, where I stopped for a few moments to smoke a cigarette at one of the tables outside, at Armenonville.

None of the laughing women there could be the lady I sought; and as my refusing to command anything caused the waiter uneasiness, in spite of my prosperous appearance, I remained but a few moments, then trudged on, all the long way to the Cafe' de Madrid, where also she was not.

How did I assure myself of this since I had not seen her face? I cannot tell you. Perhaps I should not have known her; but that night I was sure that I should.

Yes, as sure of that as I was sure that she was beautiful!

CHAPTER THREE

Early the whole of the next day, endeavoring to look preoccupied, I haunted the lobbies and vicinity of the most expensive hotels, unable to do any other thing, but ashamed of myself that I had not returned to my former task of seeking employment, although still reassured by possession of two louis and some silver, I dined well at a one-franc coachman's restaurant, where my elegance created not the slightest surprise, and I felt that I might live in this way indefinitely.

However, dreams often conclude abruptly, and two louis always do, as I found, several days later, when, after paying the rent for my unspeakable lodging and lending twenty francs to a poor, bad painter, whom I knew and whose wife was ill, I found myself with the choice of obtaining funds on my finery or not eating, either of which I was very loath to do. It is not essential for me to tell any person that when you seek a position it is better that you appear not too greatly in need of it; and my former garments had prejudiced many against me, I fear, because they had been patched by a friendly concierge. Pantaloons suffer as terribly as do antiques from too obvious restorations; and while I was only grateful to the good woman's needle (except upon one occasion when she forgot to remove it), my costume had reached, at last, great sympathies for the shade of Praxiteles, feeling the same melancholy over original intentions so far misrepresented by renewals.

Therefore I determined to preserve my fineries to the uttermost; and it was fortunate that I did so; because, after dining, for three nights upon nothing but looking out of my window, the fourth morning brought me a letter from my English friend. I had written to him, asking if he knew of any people who wished to pay a salary to a young man who knew how to do nothing. I place his reply in direct annexation:

"Henrietta Street, Cavendish Square, May 14.

"My dear Ansolini, - Why haven't you made some of your relatives do something? I understand that they do not like you; neither do my own, but after our crupper at Monte Carlo what could mine do, except provide? If a few pounds (precious few, I fear!) be of any service to you, let me know. In the mean time, if you are serious about a position, I may, preposterously enough, set you in the way of it. There is an old thundering Yankee here, whom I met in the States, and who believed me a god because I am the nephew of my awful uncle, for whose career he has ever had, it appears, a life-long admiration, sir! Now, by chance, meeting this person in the street, it developed that he had need of a man, precisely such a one as you are not: a sober, tutorish, middle-aged, dissenting parson, to trot about the Continent tied to a dancing bear. It is the old gentleman's cub, who is a species of Caliban in fine linen, and who has taken a few too many liberties in the land of the free. In fact, I believe he is much a youth of my own kind with similar admiration for baccarat and good cellars. His father must return at once, and has decided (the cub's native heath and friends being too wild) to leave him in charge of a proper guide, philosopher, courier, chaplain, and friend, if such can be found, the same required to travel with the cub and keep him out of mischief. I thought of your letter directly, and I have given you the most tremendous recommendation - part of it quite true, I suspect, though I am not a judge of learning. I explained, however, that you are a master of languages, of elegant though subdued deportment, and I extolled at length your saintly habits. Altogether, I fear there may have been too much of the virtuoso in my interpretation of you; few would have recognized from it the gentleman who closed a table at Monte Carlo and afterwards was closed himself in the handsome and spectacular fashion I remember with both delight and regret. Briefly, I lied like a master. He almost had me in the matter of your age; it was important that you should be middle-aged. I swore that you were at least thirty-eight, but, owing to exemplary habits, looked very much younger. The cub himself is twenty-four.

"Hence, if you are really serious and determined not to appeal to your people, call at once upon Mr. Lambert R. Poor, of the Hotel d'Iena. He is the father, and the cub is with him. The elder Yankee is primed with my praises of you, and must engage someone at once, as he sails in a day or two. Go - with my blessing, an air of piety, and as much age as you can assume. When the father has departed, throw the cub into the Seine, but preserve his pocket-book, and we shall have another go at those infernal tables. Vale! J.G.S."

I found myself smiling - I fear miserably - over this kind letter, especially at the wonder of my friend that I had not appealed to my relatives. The only ones who would have liked to help me, if they had known I needed something, were my two little nieces who were in my own care; because my father, being but a poet, had no family, and my mother had lost hers, even her eldest son, by marrying my father. After that they would have nothing to do with her, nor were they asked. That rascally old Antonio was now the head of all the Caravacioli, as was I of my own outcast branch of our house - that is, of my two little nieces and myself. It was partly of these poor infants I had thought when I took what was left of my small inheritance to Monte Carlo, hoping, since I seemed to be incapable of increasing it in any other way, that number seventeen and black would hand me over a fortune as a waiter does wine. Alas! Luck is not always a fool's servant, and the kind of fortune she handed me was of that species the waiter brings you in the other bottle of champagne, the gold of a bubbling brain, lasting an hour. After this there is always something evil to one's head, and mine, alas! was shaved.

Half an hour after I had read the letter, the little paper-flower makers in the attic window across from mine may have seen me shaving it - without pleasure - again. What else was I to do? I could not well expect to be given the guardianship of an erring young man if I presented myself to his parent as a gentleman who had been sitting at the Cafe' de la Paix with his head painted. I could not wear my hat through the interview. I could not exhibit the thick five days' stubble, to appear in contrast with the heavy fringe that had been spared; - I could not trim the fringe to the shortness of the stubble; I should have looked like Pierrot. I had only, then, to remain bald, and, if I obtained the post, to shave in secret - a harmless and mournful imposition.

It was well for me that I came to this determination. I believe it was the appearance of maturity which my head and dining upon thoughts lent me, as much as my friend's praises, which created my success with the amiable Mr. Lambert R. Poor. I witness that my visit to him provided one of the most astonishing interviews of my life. He was an instance of those strange beings of the Western republic, at whom we are perhaps too prone to pass from one of ourselves to another the secret smile, because of some little imperfections of manner. It is a type which has grown more and more familiar to us, yet never less strange: the man in costly but severe costume, big, with a necessary great waist-coat, not noticing the loudness of his own voice; as ignorant of the thousand tiny things which we observe and feel as he would be careless of them (except for his wife) if he knew. We laugh at him, sometimes even to his face, and he does not perceive it. We are a little afraid that he is too large to see it; hence too large for us to comprehend, and in spite of our laughter we are always conscious of a force - yes, of a presence! We jeer slyly, but we respect, fear a little, and would trust.

Such was my patron. He met me with a kind greeting, looked at me very earnestly, but smiling as if he understood my good intentions, as one understands the friendliness of a capering poodle, yet in such a way that I could not feel resentment, for I could see that he looked at almost everyone in the same fashion.

My friend had done wonders for me; and I made the best account of myself that I could, so that within half an hour it was arranged that I should take charge of his son, with an honourarium which gave me great rejoicing for my nieces and my accumulated appetite.

"I think I can pick men," he said, "and I think that you are the man I want. You're old enough and you've seen enough, and you know enough to keep one fool boy in order for six months."

So frankly he spoke of his son, yet not without affection and confidence. Before I left, he sent for the youth himself, Lambert R. Poor, Jr., - not at all a Caliban, but a most excellent-appearing, tall gentleman, of astonishingly meek countenance. He gave me a sad, slow look from his blue eyes at first; then with a brightening smile he gently shook my hand, murmuring that he was very glad in the prospect of knowing me better; after which the parent defined before him, with singular elaboration, my duties. I was to correct all things in his behaviour which I considered improper or absurd. I was to dictate the line of travel, to have a restraining influence upon expenditures; in brief, to control the young man as a governess does a child.

To all of his parent's instructions Poor Jr. returned a dutiful nod and expressed perfect acquiescence. The following day the elder sailed from Cherbourg, and I took up my quarters with the son.

CHAPTER FOUR

It is with the most extreme mortification that I record my ensuing experiences, for I felt that I could not honourably accept my salary without earning it by carrying out the parent Poor's wishes. That first morning I endeavoured to direct my pupil's steps toward the Musee de Cluny, with the purpose of inciting him to instructive study; but in the mildest, yet most immovable manner, he proposed Longchamps and the races as a substitute, to conclude with dinner at La Cascade and supper at Maxim's or the Cafe' Blanche, in case we should meet engaging company. I ventured the vainest efforts to reason with him, making for myself a very uncomfortable breakfast, though without effect upon him of any visibility. His air was uninterruptedly mild and modest; he rarely lifted his eyes, but to my most earnest argument replied only by ordering more eggs and saying in a chastened voice:

"Oh no; it is always best to begin school with a vacation. To Longchamps - we!"

I should say at once that through this young man I soon became an amateur of the remarkable North-American idioms, of humour and incomparable brevities often more interesting than those evolved by the thirteen or more dialects of my own Naples. Even at our first breakfast I began to catch lucid glimpses of the intention in many of his almost incomprehensible statements. I was able, even, to penetrate his meaning when he said that although he was "strong for aged parent," he himself had suffered much anguish from overwork of the "earnest youth racquette" in his late travels, and now desired to "create considerable trouble for Paris."

Naturally, I did not wish to begin by antagonizing my pupil - an estrangement at the commencement would only lead to his deceiving me, or a continued quarrel, in which case I should be of no service to my kind patron, so that after a strained interval I considered it best to surrender.

We went to Longchamps.

That was my first mistake; the second was to yield to him concerning the latter part of his programme; but opposition to Mr. Poor, Jr. had a curious effect of inutility. He had not in the least the air of obstinacy, - nothing could have been less like rudeness; he neither frowned not smiled; no, he did not seem even to be insisting; on the contrary, never have I beheld a milder countenance, nor heard a pleasanter voice; yet the young man was so completely baffling in his mysterious way that I considered him unique to my experience.

Thus, when I urged him not to place large wagers in the pesage, his whispered reply was strange and simple - "Watch me!" This he conclusively said as he deposited another thousand-franc note, which, within a few moments, accrued to the French government.

Longchamps was but the beginning of a series of days

and nights which wore upon my constitution - not indeed with the intensity of mortification which my former conspicuosity had engendered, yet my sorrows were stringent. It is true that I had been, since the age of seventeen, no stranger to the gaieties and dissipations afforded by the capitals of Europe; I may say I had exhausted these, yet always with some degree of quiet, including intervals of repose. I was tired of all the great foolishnesses of youth, and had thought myself done with them. Now I found myself plunged into more uproarious waters than I had ever known I, who had hoped to begin a life of usefulness and peace, was forced to dwell in the midst of a riot, pursuing my extraordinary charge.

There is no need that I should describe those days and nights. They remain in my memory as a confusion of bad music, crowds, motor-cars and champagne of which Poor Jr. was a distributing centre. He could never be persuaded to the Louvre, the Carnavalet, or the Luxembourg; in truth, he seldom rose in time to reach the museums, for they usually close at four in the afternoon. Always with the same inscrutable meekness of countenance, each night he methodically danced the cake-walk at Maxim's or one of the Montemarte restaurants, to the cheers of acquaintances of many nationalities, to whom he offered libations with prodigal enormity. He carried with him, about the boulevards at night, in the highly powerful car he had hired, large parties of strange people, who would loudly sing airs from the Folie-Rouge (to my unhappy shudderings) all the way from the fatiguing Bal Bullier to the Cafe' de Paris, where the waiters soon became affluent.

And how many of those gaily dressed and smiling

ladies whose bright eyes meet yours on the veranda of the Theatre Marigny were provided with excessive suppers and souvenir fans by the inexhaustible Poor Jr.! He left a trail of pink hundred-franc notes behind him, like a running boy dropping paper in the English game; and he kept showers of gold louis dancing in the air about him, so that when we entered the various cafes or "American bars" a cheer (not vocal but to me of perfect audibility) went up from the hungry and thirsty and borrowing, and from the attendants. Ah, how tired I was of it, and how I endeavoured to discover a means to draw him to the museums, and to Notre Dame and the Pantheon!

And how many times did I unwillingly find myself in the too enlivening company of those pretty supper-girls, and what jokings upon his head-top did the poor bald gentleman not undergo from those same demoiselles with the bright eyes, the wonderful hats, and the fluffy dresses!

How often among those gay people did I find myself sadly dreaming of that grey pongee skirt and the beautiful heart that had understood! Should I ever see that lady? Not, I knew, alas! in the whirl about Poor Jr.! As soon look for a nun at the Cafe' Blanche!

For some reason I came to be persuaded that she had left Paris, that she had gone away; and I pictured her - a little despairingly - on the borders of Lucerne, with the white Alps in the sky above her, - or perhaps listening to the evening songs on the Grand Canal, and I would try to feel the little rocking of her gondola, making myself dream that I sat at her feet. Or I could see the grey flicker of the pongee skirt in the twilight distance of cathedral aisles with a chant sounding from

a chapel; and, so dreaming, I would start spasmo-
dically, to hear the red-coated orchestra of a cafe' blare
out into "Bedelia," and awake to the laughter and rouge
and blague which that dear pongee had helped me for a
moment to forget!

To all places, Poor Jr., though never unkindly, dragged
me with him, even to make the balloon ascent at the
Porte Maillot on a windy evening. Without
embarrassment I confess that I was terrified, that I
clung to the ropes with a clutch which frayed my
gloves, while Poor Jr. leaned back against the side of
the basket and gazed upward at the great swaying ball,
with his hands in his pockets, humming the strange
ballad that was his favourite musical composition:

"The prettiest girl I ever saw

Was sipping cider through a straw-aw-haw!"

In that horrifying basket, scrambling for a foothold
while it swung through arcs that were gulfs, I believed
that my sorrows approached a sudden conclusion, but
finding myself again upon the secure earth, I decided
to come to an understanding with the young man.

Accordingly, on the following morning, I entered his
apartment and addresses myself to Poor Jr. as severely
as I could (for, truthfully, in all his follies I had found
no ugliness in his spirit - only a good-natured and
inscrutable desire of wild amusement) reminding him
of the authority his father had deputed to me, and
having the venturesomeness to hint that the son should
show some respect to my superior age.

To my consternation he replied by inquiring if I had

shaved my head as yet that morning. I could only drop in a chair, stammering to know what he meant.

"Didn't you suppose I knew?" he asked, elevating himself slightly on his elbow from the pillow. "Three weeks ago I left my aged parent in London and ran over here for a day. I saw you at the Cafe' de la Paix, and even then I knew that it was shaved, not naturally bald. When you came here I recognized you like a shot, and that was why I was glad to accept you as a guardian. I've enjoyed myself considerably of late, and you've been the best part of it, - I think you are a wonderation! I wouldn't have any other governess for the world, but you surpass the orchestra when you beg me to respect your years! I will bet you four dollars to a lead franc piece that you are younger than I am!"

Imagine the completeness of my dismay! Although he spoke in tones the most genial, and without unkindness, I felt myself a man of tatters before him, ashamed to have him know my sorry secret, hopeless to see all chance of authority over him gone at once, and with it my opportunity to earn a salary so generous, for if I could continue to be but an amusement to him and only part of his deception of Lambert R. Poor, my sense of honour must be fit for the guillotine indeed.

I had a little struggle with myself, and I think I must have wiped some amounts of the cold perspiration from my absurd head before I was able to make an answer. It may be seen what a coward I was, and how I feared to begin again that search for employment. At last, however, I was in self-control, so that I might speak without being afraid that my voice would shake.

"I am sorry," I said. "It seemed to me that my

deception would not cause any harm, and that I might be useful in spite of it - enough to earn my living. It was on account of my being very poor; and there are two little children I must take care of. - Well, at least, it is over now. I have had great shame, but I must not have greater."

"What do you mean?" he asked me rather sharply.

"I will leave immediately," I said, going to the door. "Since I am no more than a joke, I can be of no service to your father or to you; but you must not think that I am so unreasonable as to be angry with you. A man whom you have beheld reduced to what I was, at the Cafe' de la Paix, is surely a joke to the whole world! I will write to your father before I leave the hotel and explain that I feel myself unqualified - "

"You're going to write to him why you give it up!" he exclaimed.

"I shall make no report of espionage," I answered, with, perhaps, some bitterness, "and I will leave the letter for you to read and to send, of yourself. It shall only tell him that as a man of honour I cannot keep a position for which I have no qualification."

I was going to open the door, bidding him adieu, when he called out to me.

"Look here!" he said, and he jumped out of bed in his pajamas and came quickly, and held out his hand. "Look here, Ansolini, don't take it that way. I know you've had pretty hard times, and if you'll stay, I'll get good. I'll go to the Louvre with you this afternoon; we'll dine at one of the Duval restaurants, and go to that new religious tragedy afterwards. If you like, we'll leave Paris to-morrow. There's a little too much movement here, maybe. For God's sake, let your hair grow, and we'll go down to Italy and study bones and ruins and delight the aged parent! - It's all right, isn't it?"

I shook the hand of that kind Poor Jr. with a feeling in my heart that kept me from saying how greatly I thanked him - and I was sure that I could do anything for him in the world!

CHAPTER FIVE

Three days later saw us on the pretty waters of Lake Leman, in the bright weather when Mont Blanc heaves his great bare shoulders of ice miles into the blue sky, with no mist-cloak about him.

Sailing that lake in the cool morning, what a contrast to the champagne houpla nights of Paris! And how docile was my pupil! He suffered me to lead him through the Castle of Chillon like a new-born lamb, and even would not play the little horses in the Kursaal at Geneva, although, perhaps, that was because the stakes were not high enough to interest him. He was nearly always silent, and, from the moment of our departure from Paris, had fallen into dreamfulness, such as would come over myself at the thought of the beautiful lady. It touched my heart to find how he was ready with acquiescence to the slightest suggestion of mine, and, if it had been the season, I am almost credulous that I could have conducted him to Baireuth to hear Parsifal!

There were times when his mood of gentle sorrow was so like mine that I wondered if he, too, knew a grey pongee skirt. I wondered over this so much, and so marvellingly, also, because of the change in him, that at last I asked him.

We had gone to Lucerne; it was clear moonlight, and we smoked on our little balcony at the Schweitzerhof, puffing our small clouds in the enormous face of the strangest panorama of the world, that august disturbation of the earth by gods in battle, left to be a land of tragic fables since before Pilate was there, and remaining the same after William Tell was not. I sat looking up at the mountains, and he leaned on the rail, looking down at the lake. Somewhere a woman was singing from Pagliacci, and I slowly arrived at a consciousness that I had sighed aloud once or twice, not so much sadly, as of longing to see that lady, and that my companion had permitted similar sounds to escape him, but more mournfully. It was then that I asked him, in earnestness, yet with the manner of making a joke, if he did not think often of some one in North America.

"Do you believe that could be, and I making the disturbance I did in Paris?" he returned.

"Yes," I told him, "if you are trying to forget her."

"I should think it might look more as if I were trying to forget that I wasn't good enough for her and that she knew it!"

He spoke in a voice which he would have made full of ease - "off-hand," as they say; but he failed to do so.

"That was the case?" I pressed him, you see, but smilingly.

"Looks a good deal like it," he replied, smoking much at once.

"So? But that is good for you, my friend!"

"Probably." He paused, smoking still more, and then said, "It's a benefit I could get on just as well without."

"She is in North America?"

"No; over here."

"Ah! Then we will go where she is. That will be even better for you! Where is she?"

"I don't know. She asked me not to follow her. Somebody else is doing that."

The young man's voice was steady, and his face, as usual, showed no emotion, but I should have been an Italian for nothing had I not understood quickly. So I waited for a little while, then spoke of old Pilatus out there in the sky, and we went to bed very late, for it was out last night in Lucerne.

Two days later we roared our way out of the gloomy St. Gotthard and wound down the pass, out into the sunshine of Italy, into that broad plain of mulberries where the silkworms weave to enrich the proud Milanese. Ah, those Milanese! They are like the people of Turin, and look down upon us of Naples; they find us only amusing, because our minds and movements are too quick for them to understand. I have no respect for the Milanese, except for three things: they have a cathedral, a picture, and a dead man.

We came to our hotel in the soft twilight, with the air so balmy one wished to rise and float in it. This was the hour for the Cathedral; therefore, leaving Leonardo and his fresco for the to-morrow, I conducted my uncomplaining ward forth, and through that big arcade of which the people are so proud, to the Duomo. Poor Jr. showed few signs of life as we stood before that immenseness; he said patiently that it resembled the postals, and followed me inside the portals with languor.

It was all grey hollowness in the vast place. The windows showed not any colour nor light; the splendid pillars soared up into the air and disappeared as if they mounted to heights of invisibility in the sky at night. Very far away, at the other end of the church it seemed, one lamp was burning, high over the transept. One could not see the chains of support nor the roof above it; it seemed a great star, but so much all alone. We walked down the long aisle to stand nearer to it, the darkness growing deeper as we advanced. When we came almost beneath, both of us gazing upward, my companion unwittingly stumbled against a lady who was standing silently looking up at this light, and who had failed to notice our approach. The contact was severe enough to dislodge from her hand her folded parasol, for which I began to grope.

There was a hurried sentence of excusation from Poor Jr., followed by moments of silence before she replied. Then I heard her voice in startled exclamation:

"Rufus, it is never you?"

He called out, almost loudly,

"Alice!"

Then I knew that it was the second time I had lifted a

parasol from the ground for the lady of the grey pongee and did not see her face; but this time I placed it in her own hand; for my head bore no shame upon it now.

In the surprise of encountering Poor Jr. I do not think she noticed that she took the parasol or was conscious of my presence, and it was but too secure that my young friend had forgotten that I lived. I think, in truth, I should have forgotten it myself, if it had not been for the leaping of my heart.

Ah, that foolish dream of mine had proven true: I knew her, I knew her, unmistaking, without doubt or hesitancy - and in the dark! How should I know at the mere sound of her voice? I think I knew before she spoke!

Poor Jr. had taken a step toward her as she fell back; I could only see the two figures as two shadows upon shadow, while for them I had melted altogether and was forgotten.

"You think I have followed you," he cried, "but you have no right to think it. It was an accident and you've got to believe me!"

"I believe you," she answered gently. "Why should I not?"

"I suppose you want me to clear out again," he went on, "and I will; but I don't see why."

Her voice answered him out of the shadow: "It is only you who make a reason why. I'd give anything to be friends with you; you've always known that."

"Why can't we be?" he said, sharply and loudly. "I've changed a great deal. I'm very sensible, and I'll never bother you again - that other way. Why shouldn't I see a little of you?"

I heard her laugh then - happily, it seemed to me, - and I thought I perceived her to extend her hand to him, and that he shook it briefly, in his fashion, as if it had been the hand of a man and not that of the beautiful lady.

"You know I should like nothing better in the world - since you tell me what you do," she answered.

"And the other man?" he asked her, with the same hinting of sharpness in his tone. "Is that all settled?"

"Almost. Would you like me to tell you?"

"Only a little - please!"

His voice had dropped, and he spoke very quietly, which startlingly caused me to realize what I was doing. I went out of hearing then, very softly. Is it creible that I found myself trembling when I reached the twilit piazza? It is true, and I knew that never, for one moment, since that tragic, divine day of her pity, had I wholly despaired of beholding her again; that in my most sorrowful time there had always been a little, little morsel of certain knowledge that I should some day be near her once more.

And now, so much was easily revealed to me: it was to see her that the good Lambert R. Poor Jr., had come to Paris, preceding my patron; it was he who had passed with her on the last day of my shame, and whom she had addressed by his central name of Rufus, and it was to his hand that I had restored her parasol.

I was to look upon her face at last - I knew it - and to speak with her. Ah, yes, I did tremble! It was not because I feared she might recognize her poor slave of the painted head-top, nor that Poor Jr. would tell her. I knew him now too well to think he would do that, had I been even that other of whom he had spoken, for he was a brave, good boy, that Poor Jr. No, it was a trembling of another kind - something I do not know how to explain to those who have not trembled in the same way; and I came alone to my room in the hotel, still trembling a little and having strange quickness of breathing in my chest.

I did not make any light; I did not wish it, for the precious darkness of the Cathedral remained with me - magic darkness in which I beheld floating clouds made of the dust of gold and vanishing melodies. Any person who knows of these singular things comprehends how little of them can be told; but to those people who do not know of them, it may appear all great foolishness. Such people are either too young, and they must wait, or too old - they have forgotten!

It was an hour afterward, and Poor Jr. had knocked twice at my door, when I lighted the room and opened it to him. He came in, excitedly flushed, and, instead of taking a chair, began to walk quickly up and down the floor.

"I'm afraid I forgot all about you, Ansolini," he said, "but that girl I ran into is a - a Miss Landry, whom I have known a long -"

I put my hand on his shoulder for a moment and said:

"I think I am not so dull, my friend!"

He made a blue flash at me with his eyes, then smiled and shook his head.

"Yes, you are right," he answered, re-beginning his fast pace over the carpet. "It was she that I meant in Lucerne - I don't see why I should not tell you. In Paris she said she didn't want me to see her again until I could be - freiendly - the old way instead of something considerably different, which I'd grown to be. Well, I've just told her not only that I'd behave like a friend, but that I'd changed and felt like one. Pretty much of a lie that was!" He laighed, without any amusement. "But it was successful, and I suppose I can keep it up. At any rate we're going over to Venice with her and her mother to-morrow. Afterwards, we'll see them in Naples just before they sail."

"To Venice with them!" I could not repress crying out.

"Yes; we join parties for two days," he said, and stopped at a window and looked out attentively at nothing before he went on: "It won't be very long, and I don't suppose it will ever happen again. The other man is to meet them in Rome. He's a countryman of yours, and I believe - I believe it's - about - settled!"

He pronounced these last words in an even voice, but how slowly! Not more slowly than the construction of my own response, which I heard myself making:

"This countryman of mine - who is he?"

"One of your kind of Kentucky Colonels," Poor Jr. laughed mournfully. At first I did not understand; then it came to me that he had sometimes previously spoken in that idiom of the nobles, and that it had been his custom to address one of his Parisian followers, a vicomte, as "Colonel."

"What is his name?"

"I can't pronounce it, and I don't know how to spell it," he answered. "And that doesn't bring me to the verge of the grave! I can bear to forget it, at least until we get to Naples!"

He turned and went to the door, saying, cheerfully: "Well, old horse-thief" (such had come to be his name for me sometimes, and it was pleasant to hear), "we must be dressing. They're at this hotel, and we dine with them to-night."

CHAPTER SIX

How can I tell of the lady of the pongee - now that I beheld her? Do you think that, when she came that night to the salon where we were awaiting her, I hesitated to lift my eyes to her face because of a fear that it would not be so beautiful as the misty sweet face I had dreamed would be hers? Ah, no! It was the beauty which was in her heart that had made me hers; yet I knew that she was beautiful. She was fair, that is all I can tell. I cannot tell of her eyes, her height, her mouth; I saw her through those clouds of the dust of gold - she was all glamour and light. It was to be seen that everyone fell in love with her at once; that the chef d'orchestre came and played to her; and the waiters - you should have observed them! - made silly, tender faces through the great groves of flowers with which Poor Jr. had covered the table. It was most difficult for me to address her, to call her "Miss Landry." It seemed impossible that she should have a name, or that I should speak to her except as "you."

Even, I cannot tell very much of her mother, except that she was adorable because of her adorable relationship. She was florid, perhaps, and her conversation was of commonplaces and echoes, like my own, for I could not talk. It was Poor Jr. who made the talking, and in spite of the spell that was on me, I found myself full of admiration and sorrow for that brave fellow. He was all gaieties and little stories in a way I had never heard before; he kept us in quiet laughter; in a word, he was charming. The beautiful lady seemed content to listen with the greatest pleasure. She talked very little, except to encourage the young man to continue. I do not think she was brilliant, as they call it, or witty. She was much more than that in her comprehension, in her kindness - her beautiful kindness!

She spoke only once directly to me, except for the little things one must say. "I am almost sure I have met you, Signor Ansolini."

I felt myself burning up and knew that the conflagration was visible. So frightful a blush cannot be prevented by will-power, and I felt it continuing in hot waves long after Poor Jr. had effected salvation for me by a small joke upon my cosmopolitanism.

Little sleep visited me that night. The darkness of my room was luminous and my closed eyes became painters, painting so radiantly with divine colours - painters of wonderful portraits of this lady. Gallery after gallery swam before me, and the morning brought only more!

What a ride it was to Venice that day! What magical airs we rode through, and what a thieving old trickster was time, as he always becomes when one wishes hours to be long! I think Poor Jr. had made himself forget everything except that he was with her and that he must be a friend. He committed a thousand ridiculousnesses at the stations; he filled one side of the compartment with the pretty chianti-bottles, with terrible cakes, and with fruits and flowers; he never ceased his joking, which had no tiresomeness in it, and he made the little journey one of continuing, happy laughter.

And that evening another of my foolish dreams came true! I sat in a gondola with the lady of the grey pongee to hear the singing on the Grand Canal; - not, it is true, at her feet, but upon a little chair beside her mother. It was my place - to be, as I had been all day, escort to the mother, and guide and courier for that small party. Contented enough was I to accept it! How could I have hoped that the Most Blessed Mother would grant me so much nearness as that? It was not happiness that I felt, but something so much more precious, as though my heart- strings were the strings of a harp, and sad, beautiful arpeggios ran over them.

I could not speak much that evening, nor could Poor Jr. We were very silent and listened to the singing, our gondola just touching the others on each side, those in turn touching others, so that a musician from the barge could cross from one to another, presenting the hat for contributions. In spite of this extreme propinquity, I feared the collector would fall into the water when he received the offering of Poor Jr. It was "Gra-a-az', Milor! Graz'!" a hundred times, with bows and grateful smiles indeed!

It is the one place in the world where you listen to a bad voice with pleasure, and none of the voices are good - they are harsh and worn with the night-singing - yet all are beautiful because they are enchanted.

They sang some of our own Neapolitan songs that night, and last of all the loveliest of all, "La Luna Nova." It was to the cadence of it that our gondoliers moved us out of the throng, and it still drifted on the water as we swung, far down, into sight of the lights of the Ledo:

"Luna d'ar-gen-to fal-lo so-gnar -

Ba-cia-lo in fron-te non lo de-star. . . ."

Not so sweetly came those measures as the low voice of the beautiful lady speaking them.

"One could never forget it, never!" she said. "I might hear it a thousand other times and forget them, but never this first time."

I perceived that Poor Jr. turned his face abruptly toward hers at this, but he said nothing, by which I understood not only his wisdom but his forbearance.

"Strangely enough," she went on, slowly, "that song reminded me of something in Paris. Do you remember" - she turned to Poor Jr. - "that poor man we saw in front of the Cafe' de la Paix with the sign painted upon his head?"

Ah, the good-night, with its friendly cloak! The good, kind night!

"I remember," he answered, with some shortness. "A little faster, boatman!"

"I don't know what made it," she said, "I can't account for it, but I've been thinking of him all through that last song."

Perhaps not so strange, since one may know how wildly that poor devil had been thinking of her!

"I've thought of him so often," the gentle voice went on. "I felt so sorry for him. I never felt sorrier for any one in my life. I was sorry for the poor, thin cab-horses in Paris, but I was sorrier for him. I think it was the saddest sight I ever saw. Do you suppose he still has to do that, Rufus?"

"No, no," he answered, in haste. "He'd stopped before I left. He's all right, I imagine. Here's the Danieli."

She fastened a shawl more closely about her mother, whom I, with a ringing in my ears, was trying to help up the stone steps. "Rufus, I hope," the sweet voice continued, so gently, - "I hope he's found something to do that's very grand! Don't you? Something to make up to him for doing that!"

She had not the faintest dream that it was I. It was just her beautiful heart.

The next afternoon Venice was a bleak and empty setting, the jewel gone. How vacant it looked, how vacant it was! We made not any effort to penetrate the galleries; I had no heart to urge my friend. For us the whole of Venice had become one bridge of sighs, and we sat in the shade of the piazza, not watching the pigeons, and listening very little to the music. There are times when St. Mark's seems to glare at you with Byzantine cruelty, and Venice is too hot and too cold. So it was then. Evening found us staring out at the Adriatic from the terrace of a cafe' on the Ledo, our coffee cold before us. Never was a greater difference than that in my companion from the previous day. Yet he was not silent. He talked of her continually, having found that he could talk of her to me - though certainly he did not know why it was or how. He told me, as we sat by the grey- growing sea, that she had spoken of me.

"She liked you, she liked you very much," he said. "She told me she liked you because you were quiet and melancholy. Oh Lord, though, she likes everyone, I suppose! I believe I'd have a better chance with her if I hadn't always known her. I'm afraid that this damn Italian - I beg your pardon, Ansolini! -"

"Ah, no," I answered. "It is sometimes well said."

"I'm afraid his picturesqueness as a Kentucky Colonel appeals to her too much. And then he is new to her - a new type. She only met him in Paris, and he had done some things in the Abyssinian war -"

"What is his rank?" I asked.

"He's a prince. Cheap down this way; aren't they? I only hope" - and Poor Jr. made a groan - "it isn't going to be the old story - and that he'll be good to her if he gets her."

"Then it is not yet a betrothal?"

"Not yet. Mrs. Landry told me that Alice had liked him well enough to promise she'd give him her answer before she sailed, and that it was going to be yes. She herself said it was almost settled. That was just her way of breaking it to me, I fear."

"You have given up, my friend?"

"What else can I do? I can't go on following her, keeping up this play at second cousin, and she won't have anything else. Ever since I grew up she's been rather sorrowful over me because I didn't do anything but try to amuse myself - that was one of the reasons she couldn't care for me, she said, when I asked her. Now this fellow wins, who hasn't done anything either, except his one campaign. It's not that I ought to have her, but while I suppose it's a real fascination, I'm afraid there's a little glitter about being a princess. Even the best of our girls haven't got over that yet. Ah, well, about me she's right. I've been a pretty worthless sort. She's right. I've thought it all over. Three days before they sail we'll go down to Naples and hear the last word, and whatever it is we'll see them off on the 'Princess Irene.' Then you and I'll come north and sail by the first boat from Cherbourg.

"I - I?" I stammered.

"Yes," he said. "I'm going to make the aged parent shout with unmanly glee. I'm going to ask him to take me on as a hand. He'll take you, too. He uses something like a thousand Italians, and a man to manage them who can talk to them like a Dutch uncle is what he has always needed. He liked you, and he'll be glad to get you."

He was a good friend, that Poor Jr., you see, and I shook the hand that he offered me very hard, knowing how great would have been his embarrassment had I embraced him in our own fashion.

"And perhaps you will sail on the 'Princess Irene,' after all," I cried.

"No," he shook his head sadly, "it will not happen. I have not been worth it."

CHAPTER SEVEN

That Naples of mine is like a soiled coronet of white gems, sparkling only from far away. But I love it altogether, near or far, and my heart would have leaped to return to it for its own sake, but to come to it as we did, knowing that the only lady in the world was there. . . . Again, this is one of those things I possess no knowledge how to tell, and that those who know do know. How I had longed for the time to come, how I had feared it, how I had made pictures of it!

Yet I feared not so much as my friend, for he had a dim, small hope, and I had none. How could I have? I - a man whose head had been painted? I - for whom her great heart had sorrowed as for the thin, beaten cab-horses of Paris! Hope? All I could hope was that she might never know, and I be left with some little shred of dignity in her eyes!

Who cannot see that it was for my friend to fear? At times, with him, it was despair, but of that brave kind one loves to see - never a quiver of the lip, no winking of the eyes to keep tears back. And I, although of a people who express everything in every way, I understood what passed within him and found time to sorrow for him.

Most of all, I sorrowed for him as we waited for her on

the terrace of the Bertolini, that perch on the cliff so high that even the noises of the town are dulled and mingle with the sound of the thick surf far below.

Across the city, and beyond, we saw, from the terrace, the old mountain of the warm heart, smoking amiably, and the lights of Torre del Greco at its feet, and there, across the bay, I beheld, as I had nightly so long ago, the lamps of Castellamare, of Sorrento; then, after a stretch of water, a twinkling which was Capri. How good it was to know that all these had not taken advantage of my long absence to run away and vanish, as I had half feared they would. Those who have lived here love them well; and it was a happy thought that the beautiful lady knew them now, and shared them. I had never known quite all their loveliness until I felt that she knew it too. This was something that I must never tell her - yet what happiness there was in it!

I stood close to the railing, with a rambling gaze over this enchanted earth and sea and sky, while my friend walked nervously up and down behind me. We had come to Naples in the late afternoon, and had found a note from Mrs. Landry at our hotel, asking us for dinner. Poor Jr. had not spoken more than twice since he had read me this kind invitation, but now I heard a low exclamation from him, which let me know who was approaching; and that foolish trembling got hold of me again as I turned.

Mrs. Landry came first, with outstretched hand, making some talk excusing delay; and, after a few paces, followed the loveliest of all the world. Beside her, in silhouette against the white window lights of the hotel, I saw the very long, thin figure of a man, which, even before I recognized it, carried a certain ominousness to my mind.

Mrs. Landry, in spite of her florid contentedness, had sometimes a fluttering appearance of trivial agitations.

"The Prince came down from Rome this morning," she said nervously, and I saw my friend throw back his head like a man who declines the eye-bandage when they are going to shoot him. "He is dining with us. I know you will be glad to meet him."

The beautiful lady took Poor Jr.'s hand, more than he hers, for he seemed dazed, in spite of the straight way he stood, and it was easy to behold how white his face was. She made the presentation of us both at the same time, and as the other man came into the light, my mouth dropped open with wonder at the singular chances which the littleness of our world brings about.

"Prince Caravacioli, Mr. Poor. And this is Signor Ansolini."

It was my half-brother, that old Antonio!

CHAPTER EIGHT

Never lived any person with more possession of himself than Antonio; he bowed to each of us with the utmost amiability; and for expression - all one saw of it was a little streak of light in his eye-glass.

"It is yourself, Raffaele?" he said to me, in the politest manner, in our own tongue, the others thinking it some commonplace, and I knew by his voice that the meeting was as surprising and as cxaspcrating to him as to me.

Sometimes dazzling flashes of light explode across the eyes of blind people. Such a thing happened to my own, now, in the darkness. I found myself hot all over with a certain rashness that came to me. I felt that anything was possible if I would but dare enough.

"I am able to see that it is the same yourself!" I answered, and made the faintest eye-turn toward Miss Landry. Simultaneously bowing, I let my hand fall upon my pocket - a language which he understood, and for which (the Blessed Mother be thanked!) he perceived that I meant to offer battle immediately, though at that moment he offered me an open smile of benevolence. He knew nothing of my new cause for war; there was enough of the old!

The others were observing us.

"You have met?" asked the gentle voice of Miss Landry. "You know each other?"

"Exceedingly!" I answered, bowing low to her.

"The dinner is waiting in our own salon," said Mrs. Landry, interrupting. She led the way with Antonio to an open door on the terrace where servants were attending, and such a forest of flowers on the table and about the room as almost to cause her escort to stagger; for I knew, when I caught sight of them, that he had never been wise enough to send them. Neither had Poor Jr. done it out of wisdom, but because of his large way of performing everything, and his wish that loveliest things should be a background for that lady.

Alas for him! Those great jars of perfume, orchids and hyacinths and roses, almost shut her away from his vision. We were at a small round table, and she directly in opposition to him. Upon her right was Antonio, and my heart grew cold to see how she listened to him.

For Antonio could talk. At that time he spoke English even better than I, though without some knowledge of the North-American idiom which my travels with Poor Jr. had given me. He was one of those splendid egoists who seem to talk in modesty, to keep themselves behind scenes, yet who, when the curtain falls, are discovered to be the heroes, after all, though shown in so delicate a fashion that the audience flatters itself in the discovery.

And how practical was this fellow, how many years he

had been developing his fascinations! I was the only person of that small company who could have a suspicion that his moustache was dyed, that his hair was toupee, or that hints of his real age were scorpions and adders to him. I should not have thought it, if I had not known it. Here was my advantage: I had known his monstrous vanity all my life.

So he talked of himself in his various surreptitious ways until coffee came, Miss Landry listening eagerly, and my poor friend making no effort; for what were his quiet United States absurdities compared to the whole-world gaieties and Abyssinian adventures of this Othello, particularly for a young girl to whom Antonio's type was unfamiliar? For the first time I saw my young man's brave front desert him. His mouth drooped, and his eyes had an appearance of having gazed long at a bright light. I saw that hc, unhappy one, was at last too sure what her answer would be.

For myself, I said very little - I waited. I hoped and believed Antonio would attack me in his clever, disguised way, for he had always hated me and my dead brother, and he had never failed to prove himself too skilful for us. In my expectancy of his assault there was no mistake. I comprehended Antonio very well, and I knew that he feared I might seek to do him an injury, particularly after my inspired speech and gesture upon the terrace. Also, I felt that he would, if possible, anticipate my attempt and strike first. I was willing; for I thought myself in possession of his vulnerable point - never dreaming that he might know my own!

At last when he, with the coffee and cigarettes, took the knife in his hand, he placed a veil over the point.

He began, laughingly, with the picture of a pickpocket he had helped to catch in London. London was greatly inhabited by pickpockets, according to Antonio's declaration. Yet, he continued, it was nothing in comparison to Paris. Paris was the rendezvous, the world's home, for the criminals, adventurers, and rascals if the world, English, Spanish, South-Americans, North-Americans, - and even Italians! One must beware of people one had met in Paris!

"Of course," he concluded, with a most amiable smile, "there are many good people there also. That is not to be forgotten. If I should dare to make a risk on such a trifle, for instance, I would lay wager that you" - he nodded toward Poor Jr. - "made the acquaintance of Ansolini in Paris?"

This was of the greatest ugliness in its underneath significance, though the manner was disarming. Antonio's smile was so cheerful, his eye-glass so twinkling, that none of them could have been sure he truly meant anything harmful of me, though Poor Jr. looked up, puzzled and frowning.

Before he could answer I pulled myself altogether, as they say, and leaned forward, resting my elbows upon the table. "It is true," and I tried to smile as amiably as Antonio. "These coincidences occur. You meet all the great frauds of the world in Paris. Was it not there" - I turned to Mrs. Landry - "that you met the young Prince here?"

At this there was no mistaking that the others perceived. The secret battle had begun and was not secret. I saw a wild gleam in Poor Jr.'s eyes, as if he comprehended that strange things were to come; but, ah, the face of distress and wonder upon Mrs. Landry, who beheld the peace of both a Prince and a dinner assailed; and, alas! the strange and hurt surprise that came from the lady of the pongee! Let me not be a boastful fellow, but I had borne her pity and had adored it - I could face her wonder, even her scorn.

It was in the flash of her look that I saw my great chance and what I must try to do. Knowing Antonio, it was as if I saw her falling into the deep water and caught just one contemptuous glance from her before the waves hid her. But how much juster should that contempt have been if I had not tried to save her!

As for that old Antonio, he might have known enough to beware. I had been timid with him always, and he counted on it now, but a man who has shown a painted head-top to the people of Paris will dare a great deal.

"As the Prince says," replied Mrs. Landry, with many flutters, "one meets only the most agreeable people in Paris!"

"Paris!" I exclaimed. "Ah, that home of ingenuity! How they paint there! How they live, and how they dye - their beards!"

You see how the poor Ansolini played the buffoon. I knew they feared it was wine, I had been so silent until now; but I did not care, I was beyond care.

"Our young Prince speaks truly," I cried, raising my voice. "He is wise beyond his years, this youth! He will be great when he reaches middle age, for he knows Paris and understands North America! Like myself, he is grateful that the people of your continent enrich our own! We need all that you can give us! Where should we be - any of us" (I raised my voice still louder and waved my hand to Antonio), - "where should we be, either of us" (and I bowed to the others) "without you?"

Mrs. Landry rose with precipitousness, and the beautiful lady, very red, followed. Antonio, unmistakably stung with the scorpions I had set upon him, sprang to the door, the palest yellow man I have ever beheld, and let the ladies pass before him.

The next moment I was left alone with Poor Jr. and his hyacinth trees.

CHAPTER NINE

For several minutes neither of us spoke. Then I looked up to meet my friend's gaze of perturbation.

A waiter was proffering cigars. I took one, and waved Poor Jr.'s hand away from the box of which the waiter made offering.

"Do not remain!" I whispered, and I saw his sad perplexity. "I know her answer has not been given. Will you present him his chance to receive it - just when her sympathy must be stronger for him, since she will think he has had to bear rudeness?"

He went out of the door quickly.

I dod not smoke. I pretended to, while the waiters made the arrangements of the table and took themselves off. I sat there a long, long time waiting for Antonio to do what I hoped I had betrayed him to do.

It befell at last.

Poor Jr. came to the door and spoke in his steady voice. "Ansolini, will you come out here a moment?"

Then I knew that I had succeeded, had made Antonio afraid that I would do the thing he himself, in a panic, had already done - speak evil of another privately.

As I reached the door I heard him call out foolishly, "But Mr. Poor, I beg you -"

Poor Jr. put his hand on my shoulder, and we walked out into the dark of the terrace. Antonio was leaning against the railing, the beautiful lady standing near. Mrs. Landry had sunk into a chair beside her daughter. No other people were upon the terrace.

"Prince Caravacioli has been speaking of you," said Poor Jr., very quietly.

"Ah?" said I.

"I listened to what he said; then I told him that you were my friend, and that I considered it fair that you should hear what he had to say. I will repeat what he said, Ansolini. If I mistake anything, he can interrupt me."

Antonio laughed, and in such a way, so sincerely, so gaily, that I was frightened.

"Very good!" he cried. "I am content. Repeat all."

"He began," Poor Jr. went on, quietly, though his hand gripped my shoulder to almost painfulness, - "he began by saying to these ladies, in my presence, that we should be careful not to pick up chance strangers to dine, in Italy, and - and he went on to give me a repetition of his friendly warning about Paris. He hinted things for a while, until I asked him to say what he knew of you. Then he said he knew all about you; that you were an outcast, a left-handed member of his own family, an adventurer -"

"It is finished, my friend," I said, interrupting him, and gazed with all my soul upon the beautiful lady. Her face was as white as Antonio's or that of my friend, or as my own must have been. She strained her eyes at me fixedly; I saw the tears standing still in them, and I knew the moment had come.

"This Caravacioli is my half-brother," I said.

Antonio laughed again. "Of what kind!"

Oh, he went on so easily to his betrayal, not knowing the United-Statesians and their sentiment, as I did.

"We had the same mother," I continued, as quietly as I could. "Twenty years after this young - this somewhat young - Prince was born she divorced his father, Caravacioli, and married a poor poet, whose bust you can see on the Pincian in Rome, though he died in the cheapest hotel in Sienna when my true brother and I were children. This young Prince would have nothing to do with my mother after her second marriage and -"

"Marriage!" Antonio laughed pleasantly again. He was admirable. "This is an old tale which the hastiness of our American friend has forced us to rehearse. The marriage was never recognized by the Vatican, and there was not twenty years -"

"Antonio, it is the age which troubles you, after all!" I said, and laughed heartily, loudly, and a long time, in the most good-natured way, not to be undone as an actor.

"Twenty years," I repeated. "But what of it? Some of the best men in the world use dyes and false -"

At this his temper went away from him suddenly and completely. I had struck the right point indeed!

"You cammorrista!" he cried, and became only himself, his hands gesturing and flying, all his pleasant manner gone. "Why should we listen one second more to such a fisherman! The very seiners of the bay who sell dried sea-horses to the tourists are better gentlemen than you. You can shrug your shoulders! I saw you in Paris, though you thought I did not! Oh, I saw you well! Ah! At the Cafe de la Paiz!"

At this I cried out suddenly. The sting and surprise of it were more than I could bear. In my shame I would even have tried to drown his voice with babblings but after this one cry I could not speak for a while. He went on triumphantly:

"This rascal, my dear ladies, who has persuaded you to ask him to dinner, this camel who claims to be my excellent brother, he, for a few francs, in Paris, shaved his head and showed it for a week to the people with an advertisement painted upon it of the worst ballet in Paris. This is the gentleman with whom you ask Caravacioli to dine!"

It was beyond my expectation, so astonishing and so cruel that I could only look at him for a moment or two. I felt as one who dreams himself falling forever. Then I stepped forward and spoke, in thickness of voice, being unable to lift my head:

"Again it is true what he says. I was that man of the

painted head. I had my true brother's little daughters to care for. They were at the convent, and I owed for them. It was also partly for myself, because I was hungry. I could find not any other way, and so - but that is all."

I turned and went stumblingly away from them.

In my agony that she should know, I could do nothing but seek greater darkness. I felt myself beaten, dizzy with beatings. That thing which I had done in Paris discredited me. A man whose head-top had borne an advertisement of the Folie-Rouge to think he could be making a combat with the Prince Caravacioli!

Leaning over the railing in the darkest corner of the terrace, I felt my hand grasped secondarily by that good friend of mine.

"God bless you!" whispered Poor Jr.

"On my soul, I believe he's done himself. Listen!"

I turned. That beautiful lady had stepped out into the light from the salon door. I could see her face shining, and her eyes - ah me, how glorious they were! Antonio followed her.

"But wait," he cried pitifully.

"Not for you!" she answered, and that voice of hers, always before so gentle, rang out as the Roman trumpets once rang from this same cliff. "Not for you! I saw him there with his painted head and I under-stood! You saw him there, and you did nothing to help him! And the two little children - your nieces, too, -

and he your brother!"

Then my heart melted and I found myself choking, for the beautiful lady was weeping.

"Not for you, Prince Caravacioli," she cried, through her tears, - "Not for you!"

CHAPTER TEN

All of the beggars in Naples, I think, all of the flower-girls and boys, I am sure, and all the wandering serenaders, I will swear, were under our windows at the Vesuve, from six o'clock on the morning the "Princess Irene" sailed; and there need be no wonder when it is known that Poor Jr. had thrown handfuls of silver and five-lire notes from our balcony to strolling orchestras and singers for two nights before.

They wakened us with "Addio, la bella Napoli, addio, addio!" sung to the departing benefactor. When he had completed his toilet and his coffee, he showed himself on the balcony to them for a moment. Ah! What a resounding cheer for the signore, the great North-American nobleman! And how it swelled to a magnificent thundering when another largess of his came flying down among them!

Who could have reproved him? Not Raffaele Ansolini, who was on his knees over the bags and rugs! I think I even made some prolongation of that position, for I was far from assured of my countenance, that bright morning.

I was not to sail in the "Princess Irene" with those dear friends. Ah no! I had told them that I must go back to Paris to say good-bye to my little nieces and sail from

Boulogne - and I am sure they believed that was my reason. I had even arranged to go away upon a train which would make it not possible for me to drive to the dock with them. I did not wish to see the boat carry them away from me.

And so the farewells were said in the street in all that crowd. Poor Jr. and I were waiting at the door when the carriage galloped up. How the crowd rushed to see that lady whom it bore to us, blushing and laughing! Clouds of gold-dust came before my eyes again; she wore once more that ineffable grey pongee!

Servants ran forward with the effects of Poor Jr. and we both sprang toward the carriage.

A flower-girl was offering a great basket of loose violets. Poor Jr. seized it and threw them like a blue rain over the two ladies.

"Bravo! Bravo!"

A hundred bouquets showered into the carriage, and my friend's silver went out in another shower to meet them.

"Addio, la bella Napoli!" came from the singers and the violins, but I cried to them for "La Luna Nova."

"Good-bye - for a little while - good-bye!"

I knew how well my friend liked me, because he shook my hand with his head turned away. Then the grey glove of the beautiful lady touched my shoulder - the lightest touch in all the world - as I stood close to the carriage while Poor Jr. climbed in.

"Good-bye. Thank you - and God bless you!" she said, in a low voice. And I knew for what she thanked me.

The driver cracked his whip like an honest Neapolitan. The horses sprang forward. "Addio, addio!"

I sang with the musicians, waving and waving and waving my handkerchief to the departing carriage.

Now I saw my friend lean over and take the beautiful lady by the hand, and together they stood up in the carriage and waved their handkerchiefs to me. Then, but not because they had passed out of sight, I could see them not any longer.

They were so good - that kind Poor Jr. and the beautiful lady; they seemed like dear children - as if they had been my own dear children.

Choose from Thousands of 1stWorldLibrary Classics By

Adolphus WilliamWard
Aesop
Agatha Christie
Alexander Aaronsohn
Alexander Kielland
Alexandre Dumas
Alfred Gatty
Alfred Ollivant
Alice Duer Miller
Alice Turner Curtis
Alice Dunbar
Ambrose Bierce
Amelia E. Barr
Andrew Lang
Andrew McFarland Davis
Anna Sewell
Annie Besant
Annie Hamilton Donnell
Annie Payson Call
Anton Chekhov
Arnold Bennett
Arthur Conan Doyle
Arthur Ransome
Atticus
B. M. Bower
Basil King
Bayard Taylor
Ben Macomber
Booth Tarkington
Bram Stoker
C. Collodi
C. E. Orr
C. M. Ingleby
Carolyn Wells
Catherine Parr Traill
Charles A. Eastman
Charles Dickens
Charles Dudley Warner
Charles Farrar Browne
Charles Ives
Charles Kingsley
Charles Lathrop Pack
Charles Whibley
Charles Willing Beale
Charlotte M. Braeme
Charlotte M.Yonge
Clair W. Hayes
Clarence Day Jr.
Clarence E. Mulford

Clemence Housman
Confucius
Cornelis DeWitt Wilcox
Cyril Burleigh
D. H. Lawrence
Daniel Defoe
David Garnett
Don Carlos Janes
Donald Keyhole
Dorothy Kilner
Dougan Clark
E. Nesbit
E.P.Roe
E. Phillips Oppenheim
Edgar Allan Poe
Edgar Rice Burroughs
Edith Wharton
Edward J. O'Biren
John Cournos
Edwin L. Arnold
Eleanor Atkins
Elizabeth Cleghorn
Gaskell
Elizabeth Von Arnim
Ellem Key
Emily Dickinson
Erasmus W. Jones
Ernie Howard Pie
Ethel Turner
Ethel Watts Mumford
Eugenie Foa
Eugene Wood
Evelyn Everett-Green
Everard Cotes
F. J. Cross
Federick Austin Ogg
Ferdinand Ossendowski
Francis Bacon
Francis Darwin
Frances Hodgson Burnett
Frank Gee Patchin
Frank Harris
Frank Jewett Mather
Frank L. Packard
Frederick Trevor Hill
Frederick Winslow Taylor
Friedrich Kerst
Friedrich Nietzsche
Fyodor Dostoyevsky

Gabrielle E. Jackson
Garrett P. Serviss
Gaston Leroux
George Ade
Geroge Bernard Shaw
George Ebers
George Eliot
George MacDonald
George Orwell
George Tucker
George W. Cable
George Wharton James
Gertrude Atherton
Grace E. King
Grant Allen
Guillermo A. Sherwell
Gulielma Zollinger
Gustav Flaubert
H. A. Cody
H. B. Irving
H. G. Wells
H. H. Munro
H. Irving Hancock
H. Rider Haggard
H. W. C. Davis
Hamilton Wright Mabie
Hans Christian Andersen
Harold Avery
Harold McGrath
Harriet Beecher Stowe
Harry Houidini
Helent Hunt Jackson
Helen Nicolay
Hendy David Thoreau
Henrik Ibsen
Henry Adams
Henry Ford
Henry Frost
Henry James
Henry Jones Ford
Henry Seton Merriman
Henry Wadsworth
Longfellow
Henry W Longfellow
Herbert A. Giles
Herbert N. Casson
Herman Hesse
Homer
Honore De Balzac

Horace Walpole
Horatio Alger, Jr.
Howard Pyle
Howard R. Garis
Hugh Lofting
Hugh Walpole
Humphry Ward
Ian Maclaren
Israel Abrahams
J.G.Austin
J. Henri Fabre
J. M. Barrie
J. Macdonald Oxley
J. S. Knowles
J. Storer Clouston
Jack London
Jacob Abbott
James Allen
James Lane Allen
James Andrews
James Baldwin
James DeMille
James Joyce
James Oliver Curwood
James Oppenheim
James Otis
Jane Austen
Jens Peter Jacobsen
Jerome K. Jerome
John Burroughs
John F. Kennedy
John Gay
John Glasworthy
John Habberton
John Joy Bell
John Milton
John Philip Sousa
Jonathan Swift
Joseph Carey
Joseph Conrad
Joseph Jacobs
Julian Hawthrone
Julies Vernes
Justin Huntly McCarthy
Kakuzo Okakura
Kenneth Grahame
Kate Langley Bosher
L. A. Abbot
L. T. Meade
L. Frank Baum
Laura Lee Hope

Laurence Housman
Leo Tolstoy
Leonid Andreyev
Lewis Carroll
Lilian Bell
Lloyd Osbourne
Louis Tracy
Louisa May Alcott
Lucy Fitch Perkins
Lucy Maud Montgomery
Lydia Miller Middleton
Lyndon Orr
M. H. Adams
Margaret E. Sangster
Margaret Vandercook
Maria Edgeworth
Maria Thompson Daviess
Mariano Azuela
Marion Polk Angellotti
Mark Overton
Mark Twain
Mary Austin
Mary Cole
Mary Rowlandson
Mary Wollstonecraft
Shelley
Max Beerbohm
Myra Kelly
Nathaniel Hawthrone
O. F. Walton
Oscar Wilde
Owen Johnson
P.G.Wodehouse
Paul and Mable Thorn
Paul G. Tomlinson
Paul Severing
Peter B. Kyne
Plato
R. Derby Holmes
R. L. Stevenson
Rabindranath Tagore
Rahul Alvares
Ralph Waldo Emmerson
Rene Descartes
Rex E. Beach
Richard Harding Davis
Richard Jefferies
Robert Barr
Robert Frost
Robert Gordon Anderson
Robert L. Drake

Robert Lansing
Robert Michael Ballantyne
Robert W. Chambers
Rosa Nouchette Carey
Ross Kay
Rudyard Kipling
Samuel B. Allison
Samuel Hopkins Adams
Sarah Bernhardt
Selma Lagerlof
Sherwood Anderson
Sigmund Freud
Standish O'Grady
Stanley Weyman
Stella Benson
Stephen Crane
Stewart Edward White
Stijn Streuvels
Swami Abhedananda
Swami Parmananda
T. S. Ackland
The Princess Der Ling
Thomas A. Janvier
Thomas A Kempis
Thomas Anderton
Thomas Bailey Aldrich
Thomas Bulfinch
Thomas De Quincey
Thomas H. Huxley
Thomas Hardy
Thomas More
Thornton W. Burgess
U. S. Grant
Valentine Williams
Victor Appleton
Virginia Woolf
Walter Scott
Washington Irving
Wilbur Lawton
Wilkie Collins
Willa Cather
Willard F. Baker
William Makepeace
Thackeray
William W. Walter
Winston Churchill
Yei Theodora Ozaki
Young E. Allison
Zane Grey